Brer Rabbit

Published by The Kipling Press, Inc.
155 Sixth Avenue, New York, New York 10013
Copyright © 1988 by The Kipling Press
Text Copyright © 1988 by Mark Davies
Illustrations Copyright © 1988 by Arthur Suydam
Book Design by Michael Hortens
All Rights Reserved.

International Standard Book Number: 0-9437-1816-3
Manufactured and Printed in the United States of America

The Kipling Press Library of American Folktales

Brer Rabbit

Adapted by Mark Davies

Illustrated by Arthur Suydam

The Kipling Press ★ New York

Foreword

Who is Brer Rabbit? What does "Brer" mean, anyway? Well, Brer means Brother, and Brother—or Brer—Rabbit was the main character in many stories that were told by black slaves in the South. In these stories, Brer Rabbit is a "trickster."

Tricksters appear in stories from many different countries and cultures. American Indians have Coyote; West Africans have Spider; the Irish have the wee people, or leprechauns; and the Polynesians and New Zealanders have Maui, a person who was reared by sea creatures.

Tricksters are always animals or magical beings. Usually, they are cunning, mischievous, and lazy. They are rarely really mean or cruel. In fact, they are often smaller or less powerful than the people they trick. Sometimes they are looked down on by the rest of the characters in the story.

Stories with tricksters have always been popular. One reason is that the stories are often funny; they entertain people. But they also have another important purpose, especially for black Americans who told the stories. The trickster usually represents a human. In the story, the trickster can get away with behavior that the person would be punished for. When Brer Rabbit tricks the bigger, stronger animals in the tale, the storyteller and the listener can imagine they are Brer Rabbit and come out on top for once.

Of course, Brer Rabbit doesn't always come out on top. Sometimes he gets tricked. But if he can't outdo someone, he at least finds a way to break even. For black slaves in the South, it was important to be able to outwit their powerful white masters—even if it was only in their stories and in their imaginations.

A white journalist named Joel Chandler Harris began collecting folktales from the ex-slaves who had taken care of him when he was a boy. The stories they told him were mostly trickster tales, and Brer Rabbit was the most popular character of all.

In 1880, Harris published some of the stories he had heard from his black housekeeper. The book was called *Uncle Remus: His Songs and Stories.* He created the character of Uncle Remus, an old black man who told the tales to entertain and educate a little white boy who liked to visit his cabin. Harris tried to write the stories out just the way he heard them. He even tried to show his readers how the slaves' language sounded by spelling the words just like they were spoken. This is called writing in dialect. By writing in dialect, Harris was able to capture the poetry and rhythm of the black slaves' way of speaking.

Stories that are similar to Brer Rabbit have been heard in places far away from America. Many people believe that the stories were brought to America by African slaves. But others say the stories came to America with settlers from Europe.

But no matter where the first stories came from, Brer Rabbit is a popular American character today. Both children and adults have always enjoyed the stories about Brer Rabbit and the other Uncle Remus characters. And they will always love reading them again and again.

Sandra Dolby Stahl

Sandra Dolby Stahl
Associate Professor of Folklore and American
Studies at Indiana University

The Wonderful Tar Baby

One evening the lady whom Uncle Remus calls "Miss Sally" missed her little boy. Making a search through the house and through the yard, she heard the sound of voices in the old man's cabin and, looking through the window, saw the child sitting by Uncle Remus.

"Didn't the fox ever catch the rabbit?" asked the little boy, as he sat huddled at the old man's feet. Uncle Remus pulled thoughtfully on his scraggly, white beard before he answered.

"Now I'll tell you about one time when he come mighty near it, as sure as you're born," he replied.

One day Brer Fox went to work and got some tar, mixed it with some turpentine, and fixed up a contraption what he called a Tar-Baby. He took this Tar-Baby and sat her in the big road, and then he lay off in the bushes to see what was going to happen. He didn't have to wait long, because Brer Rabbit soon came pacing down the road—*Lippity-clippity, clippity-lippity*—just as sassy as a jay-bird. Brer Fox, he lay low.

Brer Rabbit come prancin' along till he spied the Tar-Baby, and then he stood up on his hind legs like he was astonished. The Tar-Baby, she sat there, she did, and Brer Fox, he lay low.

"Mawnin'!" says Brer Rabbit, says he. "Nice wedder this mawnin'," says he.

Tar-Baby aint sayin' nothin', and Brer Fox, he lay low. "How you feelin'?" says Brer Rabbit, says he.

Brer Fox, he wink his eye slow, and lay low, and the Tar-Baby, she aint sayin' nothin'.

"How did you get here, then? Is you deaf?" says Brer Rabbit, says he. "Cause if you is, I kin holler louder."

Tar-Baby sat still, and Brer Fox, he lay low. "You're stuck up, dat's w'at you is," says Brer Rabbit, says he, "en I'm goin' ter cure you, dat's w'at I'm goin' ter do," says he.

Brer Fox chuckled to himself, he did, but Tar-Baby aint sayin' nothin'.

"I'm goin' to teach you how ter talk ter 'spectable folks ef hit's de las' thing I do," says Brer Rabbit, says he. "Ef you don't take off dat hat and tell me howdy, I'm goin' to bust you wide open," says he.

Brer Rabbit keep on askin' her, and the Tar-Baby, she keep on sayin' nothin', till presently Brer Rabbit drew back his fists, he did, and *blip*, he hit her on the side of the head. His fist stuck and he couldn't pull loose. But Tar-Baby, she stay still, and Brer Fox, he lay low.

"Ef you don't lemme loose, I'll knock you agin," says Brer Rabbit, says he, and with that he fetched her a wipe with the other hand, and that stuck too. Tar-Baby, she aint sayin' nothin', and Brer Fox, he lay low.

"Tu'n me loose, fo' I kick de natural stuffin' outen you!" says Brer Rabbit, says he. But the Tar-Baby, she aint sayin' nothin'. She just held on, and then Brer Rabbit lost the use of his feet in the same way.

Then Brer Rabbit squall out that if the Tar-Baby didn't turn him loose, he would butt her cranksided. And then he butted, and his head got stuck. Then Brer Fox, he sauntered forth, lookin' just as innocent as one of your mama's mockin'-birds.

"Howdy, Brer Rabbit," says Brer Fox, says he. "You look sorter stuck up dis mawnin'," says he. And then he rolled on the ground, and laughed and laughed till he couldn't laugh no more.

By and by, when Brer Fox had enough of laughin' he up'n say, says he: "Well, I speck I got you dis time, Brer Rabbit," says he. "Maybe I aint, but I speck I is. You bin runnin' 'round here sassin' atter me a mighty long time, but I speck you done come ter de end er de road," says Brer Fox, says he.

"Who ax you fer ter come and strike up a 'quaintance wid dish yer Tar-Baby?" says Brer Fox, says he. "En who stuck you up dar whar you is? Nobody in de whole world but you. You just went en jam yo'se'f on dat Tar-Baby widout waitin' fer any invite, and dar you is, en dar you'll stay till I fixes up a brush-pile and fires her up, 'cause I'm goin' to bobbycue you dis dey, fo' sho," says Brer Fox, says he.

Then Brer Rabbit talk mighty humble.

"I don't keer w'at you do wid me, Brer Fox," says he, "jes so's you don't fling me in dat briar-patch. Roast me, Brer Fox," says he, "but don't fling me in dat briar-patch," says he.

"It's so much trouble fer ter kin'le a fire," says Brer Fox, says he, "dat I speck I'll hatter hang you," says he.

"Hang me jes as high as you please, Brer Fox," says Brer Rabbit, says he, "But do fer de Lord's sake don't fling me in dat briar-patch," says he.

"I aint got no string," says Brer Fox, says he, "and now I speck I'll hatter drown you," says he.

"Drown me jes as deep as you please, Brer Fox," says Brer Rabbit, says he, "but do don't fling me in dat briar-patch," says he.

"Dey aint no water nigh," says Brer Fox, says he, "and now I speck I'll hatter skin you," says he.

"Skin me, Brer Fox," says Brer Rabbit, says he, "snatch out my eyeballs, t'ar out my years by the roots, and cut off my legs," says he. "But do please, Brer Fox, don't fling me in dat briar-patch," says he.

’Cause Brer Fox wanted to hurt Brer Rabbit as bad as
he could, he caught him by the hind legs and slung
him right in the middle of the briar-patch. There was a
consider’ble flutter where Brer Rabbit struck the
bushes. Brer Fox hung round to see what was goin’ to
happen. By and by he heard somebody call him, and
way up on the hill he saw Brer Rabbit sittin’ cross-
legged on the chinkapin log, combin’ the pitch out of
his hair with a chip. Then Brer Fox knew that he had

been tricked mighty bad. Brer Rabbit was happy to fling back some of his sass, and he hollered out:

"Bawn and bred in a briar-patch, Brer Fox—bawn and bred in a briar-patch!" And with that he skipped out just as lively as a cricket in the embers.

Brer Buzzard's Gold-Mine

"Now there was someone else who managed to keep Brer Rabbit in line," said Uncle Remus, as he continued with his stories.

"I thought the Tortoise was the only one that fooled the Rabbit," said the little boy.

"It's just like I tell you, honey. If nobody had managed to fool Brer Rabbit, then they would have taken him to be a witch, and in them days they burnt witches before you could squinch your eyeballs. That's what they did."

"Who fooled the Rabbit this time?" the little boy asked, and Uncle Remus proceeded with the story.

One time Brer Rabbit and old Brer Buzzard decided to go into farming together. It was a good year, and the vegetables grew mighty well. But by and by, when the time came for sharing, it came to light that old Brer Buzzard didn't get anything. The field was empty, the vegetables all gone, and there was nothing left to show for all their hard work.

Brer Buzzard didn't say anything, but he suspected that Brer Rabbit had hidden those vegetables. He kept thinking and thinking, till one day he came along and told Brer Rabbit that he had found a rich gold-mine, just across the river.

"You come en go along wid me, Brer Rabbit," says Brer Turkey Buzzard, says he. "I'll scratch en you kin grabble, en 'tween de two un us, we'll make short wuk er dat gole-mine," said he.

Brer Rabbit was very excited about the idea, but he studied and studied how to get across the water, because every time he got his feet wet, all his family caught cold. So he asked Brer Buzzard how he was going to do it, and Brer Buzzard offered to carry Brer Rabbit across, and with that, old Brer Buzzard crouched down and spread his wings. Brer Rabbit climbed on top and up they rose.

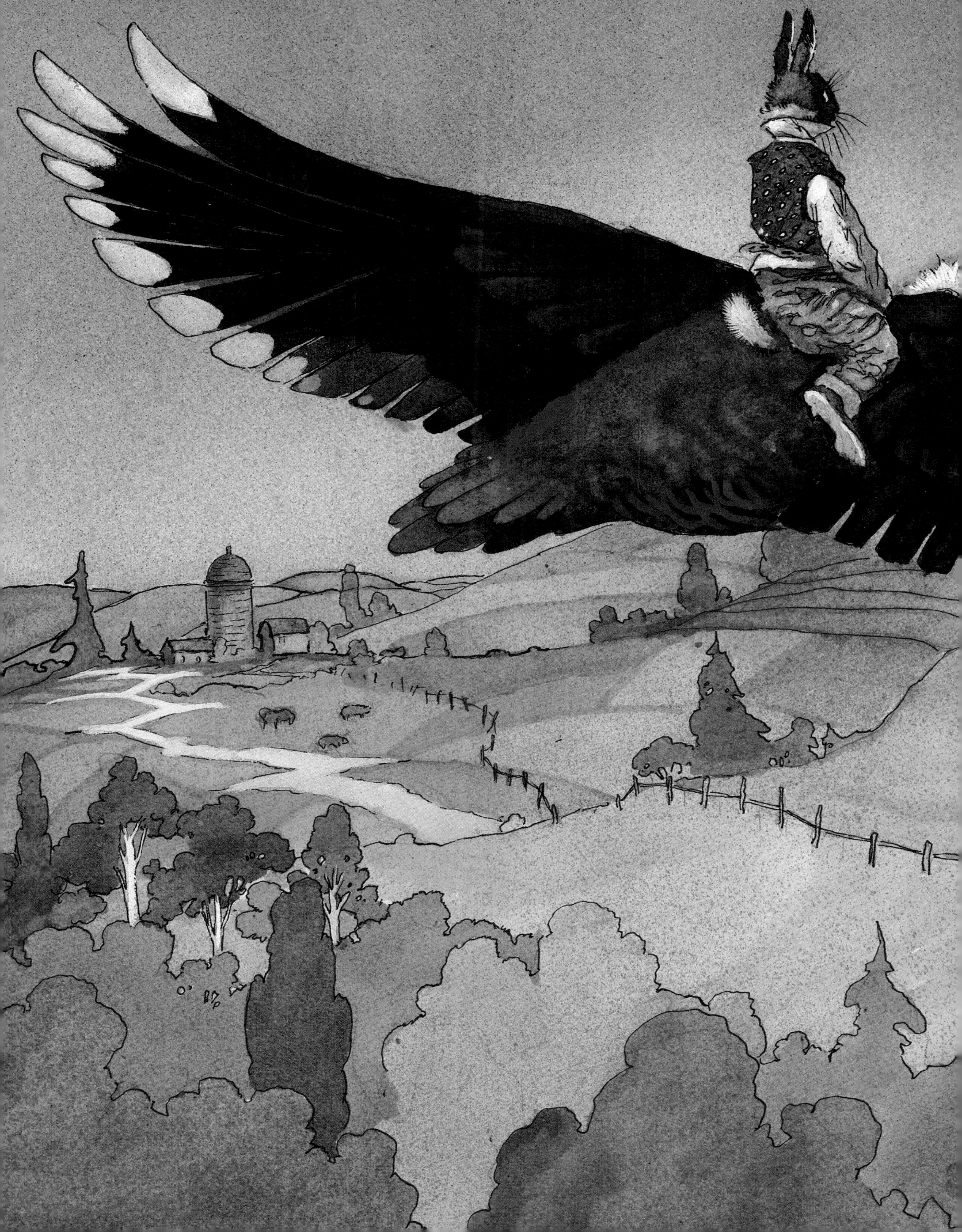

They rose, continued Uncle Remus, and when they perched, they perched in the top of the highest pine tree, and the pine that they had perched in was growin' on an island, and this island was in the middle of the river, with deep water runnin' all around. Brer Rabbit got wind of what Brer Buzzard was up to, and

became very frightened. As soon as they got balanced on a branch, Brer Rabbit climbed down from Brer Buzzard's back and said, "W'iles we're res'n here, Brer Buzzard, and being as you bin so good, I got sumpin to tell you," says he. "I got a gole-mine of my own, one w'at I make myse'f, and I speck we better go back to mine fo' we bodder 'longer wid yours," says he.

Then old Brer Buzzard laughed, and the more he laughed the more he shook, and the more he shook, the more frightened Brer Rabbit became, so Brer Rabbit

screamed out, "Hole on, Brer Buzzard! Don't flop yo'
wings w'en you laff, 'cause if you does, sumpin'll drap
fum up here, and my gole-mine won't do you no good,
and needer will yours do me no good."

"Den tell me w'at you done wid our vegetables, de
ones you bin hidin', only den will I take you back."

It didn't take long for Brer Rabbit to tell Brer
Buzzard everything, and he had to promise to share
what they had grown fair and square.
So Brer Buzzard carried him back,
and Brer Rabbit walked weak in
the knees for a month afterwards.

Brer Rabbit and the Bag in the Corner

As soon as supper was finished one evening, the little boy slipped away from the table and ran as fast as he could to the old man's cabin. Uncle Remus was sitting quietly in his chair, smoking his pipe.

"Did Brer Rabbit ever fix Brer Fox?" asked the little boy.

"Many times," the old man replied, "but there was one time when he played a mean trick on poor old Brer Fox." And so the story began.

Brer Fox was wanderin' down the big road one day, when he saw Brer Tortoise ahead, making his way home. Brer Fox thought this was a perfect opportunity to ambush Brer Tortoise, and so he rushed home to get a bag. When he returned, he ran up behind Brer Tortoise, flipped him in the bag, and slung the bag across his back.

Brer Tortoise shouted and hollered, but it didn't do any good. It wasn't long before Brer Fox had him back home and tied up in the bag in a corner.

While all this was goin' on, Brer Rabbit had been sittin' in the bushes by the side of the road, and when he saw Brer Fox go trottin' by, he asked himself what it was Brer Fox had in that there bag. He said to himself that Brer Fox had no business trottin' down the road carryin' things while other folks didn't know what they were, and he told himself that no great harm would be done if he took after Brer Fox to find out what he had in that there bag.

With that, Brer Rabbit set off. He took a short cut, and by the time Brer Fox got home, Brer Rabbit had had time to go 'round to the flower garden and do some devilment. Not long after that, he saw Brer Fox arrive with the bag slung across his back. Brer Fox lifted it off, slung Brer Tortoise down in the corner, and set down in front of the fire for a rest.

Brer Fox had hardly lit his pipe, when Brer Rabbit stuck his head in the door and hollered:

"Brer Fox! O Brer Fox! You better take yo' walkin' cane en run down here. Comin' 'long just now I hear a mighty fuss, en I look roun' en dar wuz a whole group of folks in yo' flower garden who were tramplin' around, and tarin' things down. I hollered at them, but they aint pay no 'tention ter little man like I is. Run, Brer Fox! Run!"

With that, Brer Rabbit disappeared back in the bushes, and Brer Fox dropped his pipe and grabbed his walkin' cane and set off for the flower garden; and no sooner

had he gone than old Brer Rabbit came out of the
bushes and made his way into the house.

He looked around and found the bag in the corner.
He caught hold of the bag and sort of felt it, and as he
did this, he heard somethin' shout, "Ow! Go 'way!
Lemme 'lone! Turn me loose! Ow!"

Brer Rabbit jumped back in astonishment. Then
before you could wink your eyeball, Brer Rabbit
slapped himself on the leg and broke out laughing.
"Ef I aint make no mistakes, dat ar kinder fuss kin
come fum nobody in de world but ole Brer Tortoise."

Brer Tortoise, he holler, "Aint dat Brer Rabbit?"

"De same," says he.

"Den untie me en tu'n me out. Meal dust in my
th'oat, grit in my eye, en I aint kin git my breff,
scarcely. Tu'n me out, Brer Rabbit."

Brer Tortoise talked like someone down in a well.
Brer Rabbit he holler back, "Youer lots smarter den
w'at I is, Brer Tortoise—lots smarter. Youer smarter and
cleverer. As clever as I am to be here now, youer even
smarter. I know how you git in de bag, but I
dunner how de name er goodness you tie
yo'se'f up in dar."

Brer Tortoise tried to explain, but Brer
Rabbit kept on laughin' and he laughed
until he got his fill of laughin'; then
he untied the bag and took Brer

Tortoise out and carried him way off into the woods. Then when he had done this, Brer Rabbit ran off to get a great big hornet's nest that he had seen as he was comin' along. Brer Rabbit slapped his hand across the little hole, and carried it into Brer Fox's house, and put it in the bag where Brer Tortoise had been.

Not long after, Brer Fox returned from the flower garden, and he looked like he was mighty mad. He hit the ground with his cane as though he was goin' to take his revenge out on poor old Brer Tortoise. He went in the door, Brer Fox did, and then shut it behind him. Brer Rabbit and Brer Tortoise listened in the bushes nearby, but they didn't hear nothin' yet.

Then, before you knew it, they heard the most audacious racket, to be sure. From where Brer Rabbit and Brer Tortoise were sittin', it seemed like there was a whole herd of cows running around in Brer Fox's house. They heard chairs fallin', the table turnin' over, and the crockery breakin', and then the door flew open, and out came Brer Fox, squalling as though the Old Boy was after him! Never before, and never since, had those creatures seen such a sight.

The hornets swarmed on top of Brer Fox. It looked like a dozen were stinging him at once, and that that poor creature was finding out for himself what pain and suffering was. They bit him, and they stung him, and as far as Brer Rabbit and Brer Tortoise could hear, those hornets were nailin' him!

Brer Rabbit and Brer Tortoise sat there and laughed and laughed, till after a while, Brer Rabbit rolled over and grabbed his stomach and shouted:

"Don't, Brer Tortoise! Don't! One giggle mo' en you'll hatter tote me."

Brer Rabbit and the Honey Pot

One evening Miss Sally sent a large tray of food to Uncle Remus. The little boy accompanied the bearer of the tray and remained while the old man ate supper, expecting to hear another story when he had finished. Uncle Remus paused, straightened up, looked over his spectacles at the child, and said, "I expect you want to hear 'bout the time Brer Rabbit decided to pay Brer Bear a call?"

"Why, I thought they were mad at each other," the little boy exclaimed.

"Brer Rabbit visited when Brer Bear and his family was away from home," Uncle Remus explained, with a chuckle that was in the nature of a hearty tribute to the crafty judgment of Brer Rabbit. Then he continued.

Brer Rabbit sat down by the side of the road, and he saw them go by—old Brer Bear and old Mrs. Bear, and their two twin-chilluns, Kubs and Klibs. Old Brer Bear and Mrs. Bear, they went along ahead, and Kubs and Klibs, they came shufflin' and scramblin' along behind. When Brer Rabbit saw this, he thought to himself that he had better go see how Brer Bear was getting along, an off he put.

It wasn't long before he was ransackin' their house. While he was going around peepin' in here, and pokin' in there, he got to foolin' among the shelves, and a bucket of honey that Brer Bear had hidden in the cupboard fell down and spilled all over Brer Rabbit. Just a little more and he'd have been drowned! From head to toe that creature was covered with honey. In fact, he had to sit there and let the natural sweetness drip out of his eyes before he could even see his hands before him. Then, after he looked around a little, he said to himself, he said:

"Heyo, yer! W'at I goin' to do now? Ef I go out in de sunshine, the bumbly-bees en de flies dey'll swom up'n take me. En if I stay yer, Brer Bear'll come back en ketch me, en I dunner wa't in de name er gracious I goin' to do."

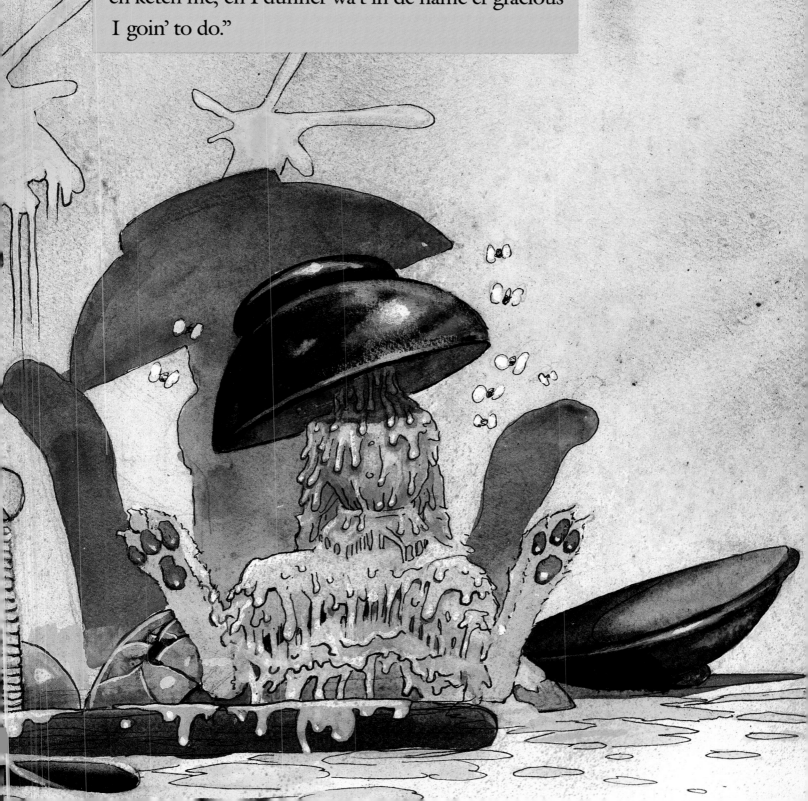

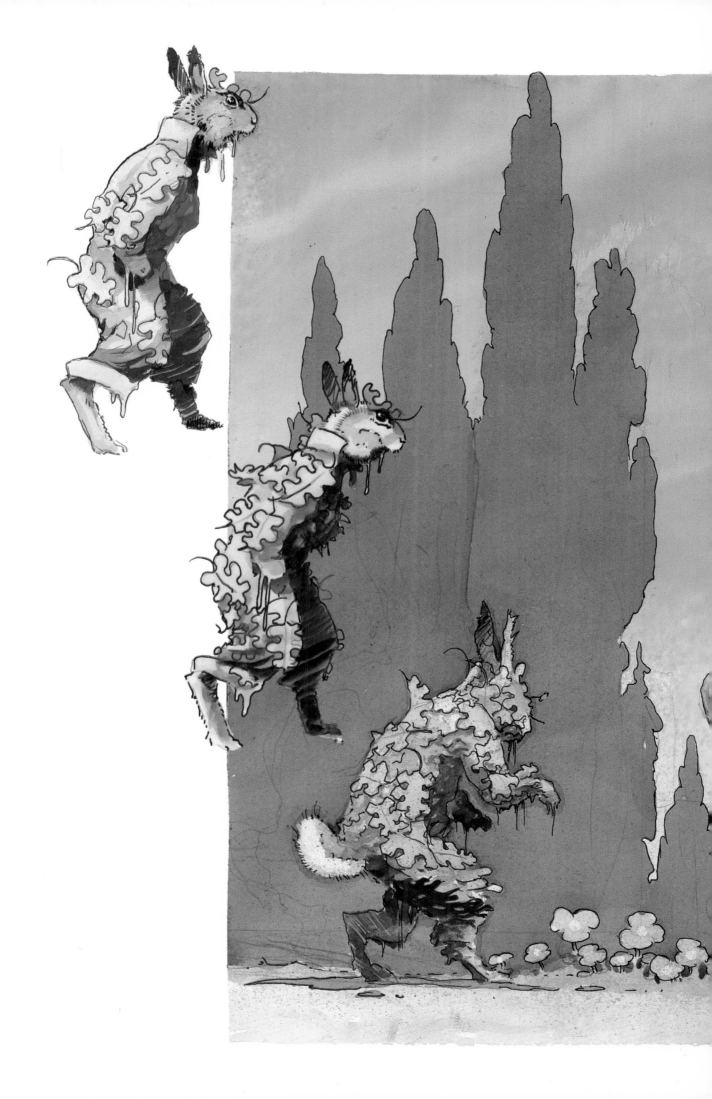

Anyway, after a while, Brer Rabbit had an idea, and he tip-toed off into the woods. As soon as he got there, he rolled in the leaves to try and rub the honey off. He rolled and rolled, but the leaves stuck to him. In fact the more he rolled, the more the leaves stuck to him, till after a while Brer Rabbit was the most audacious looking creature that you ever did see! Brer Rabbit jumped around and tried to shake the leaves off, he shook and he shivered, but the leaves still stuck. Brer Rabbit saw that this was getting him nowhere and decided to set off for home.

Brer Rabbit wandered along, and with every move he made, the leaves would go *swishy-swushy, splushy-splishy,* and, from the fuss he made and the way he looked, you'd take him to be the most savage vermin that had disappeared from the face of the earth since old man Noah let down the draw-bars of the ark and turned the animals loose.

Of course this made Brer Rabbit feel very mischievous, and so he decided to drop in on Brer Fox. He had hardly started on down the road when he came across Brer Fox and Brer Bear, who were fixing up a plan to nab Brer Rabbit. They were so deep in thought that they didn't see Brer Rabbit until he was right on them. When they caught sight of him, they became very frightened, but Brer Bear wanted to show off in front of Brer Fox and so he asked Brer

Rabbit who he was. Brer Rabbit jumped up and down in the middle of the road and hollered out:

"I'm de Wull-er-de-Wust. I'm de Wull-er-de-Wust, en you er de man I'm atter!"

Without any hesitation Brer Fox and Brer Bear picked up their feet and ran for their lives.

For a long time after that, continued Uncle Remus, whenever Brer Rabbit saw Brer Fox or Brer Bear he would hide behind a tree and holler "I'm de Wull-er-de-Wust, en you er de mens I'm, atter!"

Brer Fox and Brer Bear would flee as fast as they could, and as soon as they were out of sight and out of hearing, Brer Rabbit would show himself and laugh so hard that he'd nearly kill himself.